# I Wouldn't Be Scared

A Richard Jackson
Book

# I
# Wouldn't
# Be
# Scared

# JOHN
# SABRAW

Orchard Books    New York
A division of Franklin Watts, Inc.

Orchard Books, A division of Franklin Watts, Inc.
387 Park Avenue South, New York, NY 10016

Orchard Books Canada
20 Torbay Road, Markham, Ontario 23P 1G6

Manufactured in the United States of America
Book design by Mina Greenstein   10  9  8  7  6  5  4  3  2  1
The text of this book is set in 18 pt. ITC Quorum Medium
The illustrations are ink and watercolor paintings

Library of Congress Cataloging-in-Publication Data
Sabraw, John. I wouldn't be scared / John Sabraw.
p.   cm. "A Richard Jackson book"—Half title p.
Summary: A little boy imagines how he will conquer the monster hidden in his sewer.
ISBN 0-531-05818-2.   ISBN 0-531-08418-3 (lib. bdg.)
[1. Monsters—Fiction.   2. Fear—Fiction.]   I. Title.   PZ7.S1176Iab   1989
[E]—dc19   88-23352   CIP   AC

This book is dedicated to:

Mom

Dad

Dick

**and**

The Double D

Today I saw a beast in my backyard, and I'm going to hunt it down. It ate my dog Rusty, I think.

Well, I didn't actually see it. But I saw its tail
behind the bushes by Rusty's doghouse. When I ran over,
the tail was gone and so was Rusty.

But I saw some tracks, and they led into the sewer.
I got my stick and my boots and my coonskin cap,
and now I'm going after it.

I'm not afraid of anything, either—even if there's
a dragon in here that could barbecue me
with one fiery blast.

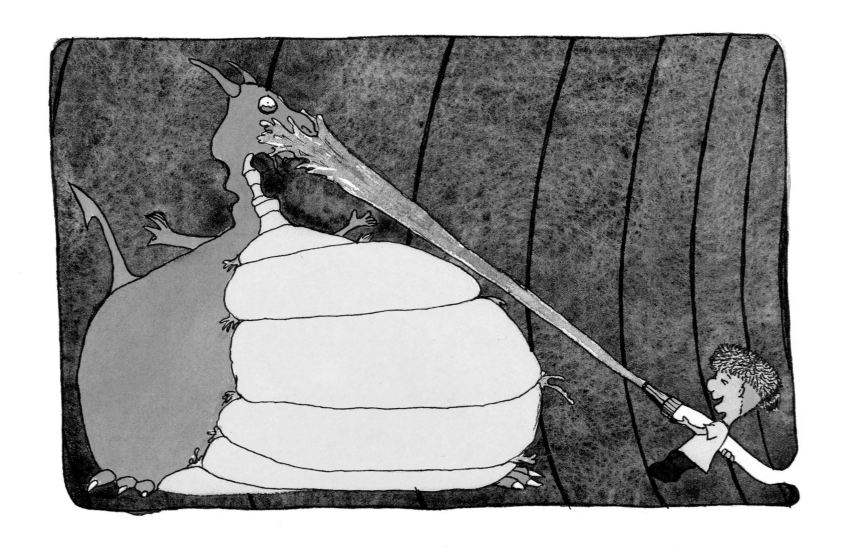

It wouldn't scare me. I'd just douse him with my hose
and put his fire out.

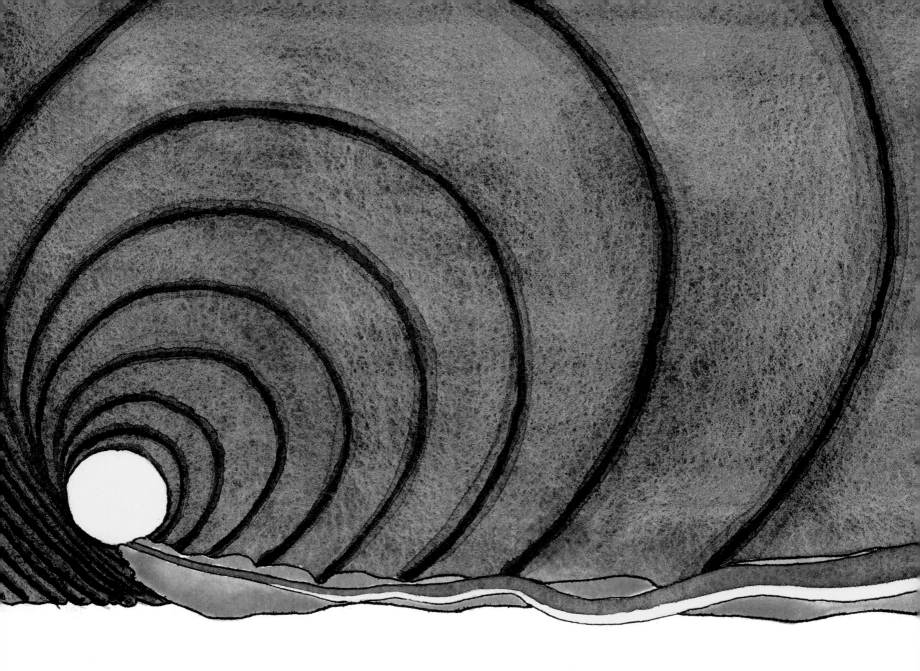

But I think it's too small in here for a dragon.

Maybe there's a slippery snake instead,
waiting to wrap himself around me and squeeze me
until I can't breathe.

I wouldn't be scared. I'd just grab him by the tail
and whip him into a big knot.

What kind of monster would go into a construction tunnel?

What if it's a giant spider inside making a web for me
so he can spin me up in his sticky silk
and turn me into a cocoon! I wouldn't be scared of that.

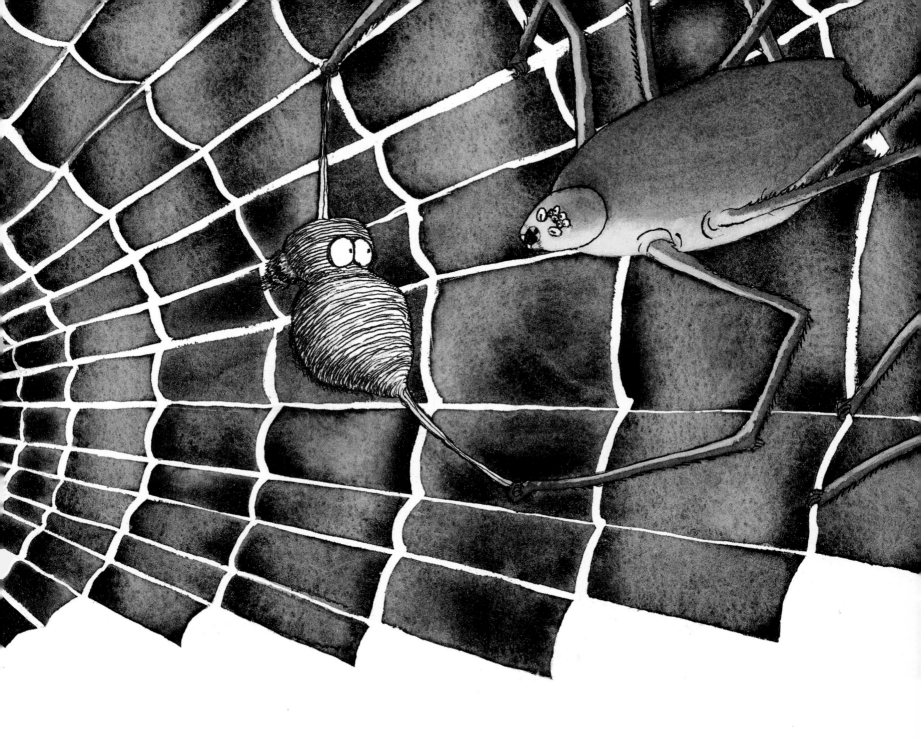

I'd swing back and forth and hypnotize him
into tangling himself all up.

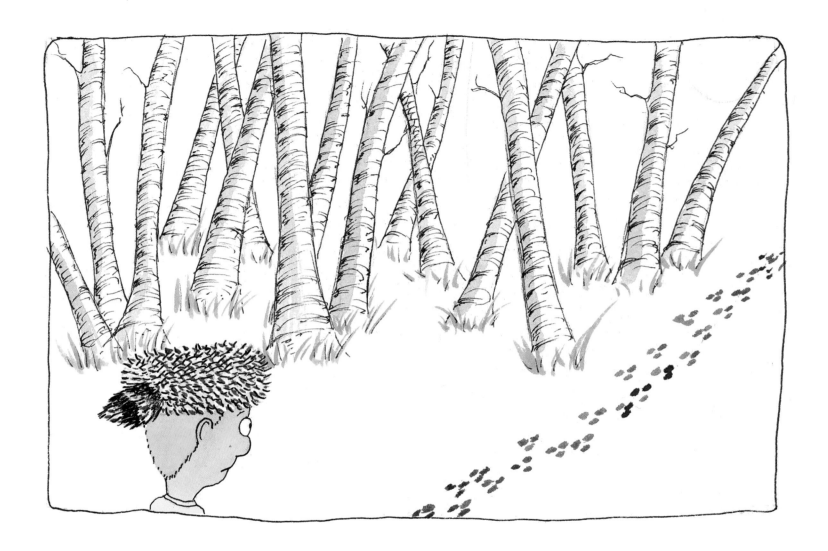

But I don't think a spider would make tracks like these....

I bet it's an angry gorilla waiting to snatch me up
and take me back to the jungle.

I wouldn't be scared. I'd get my dad's electric razor
and shave his hair until he ran off in embarrassment.

But what if it's a hungry tiger waiting to eat me whole?

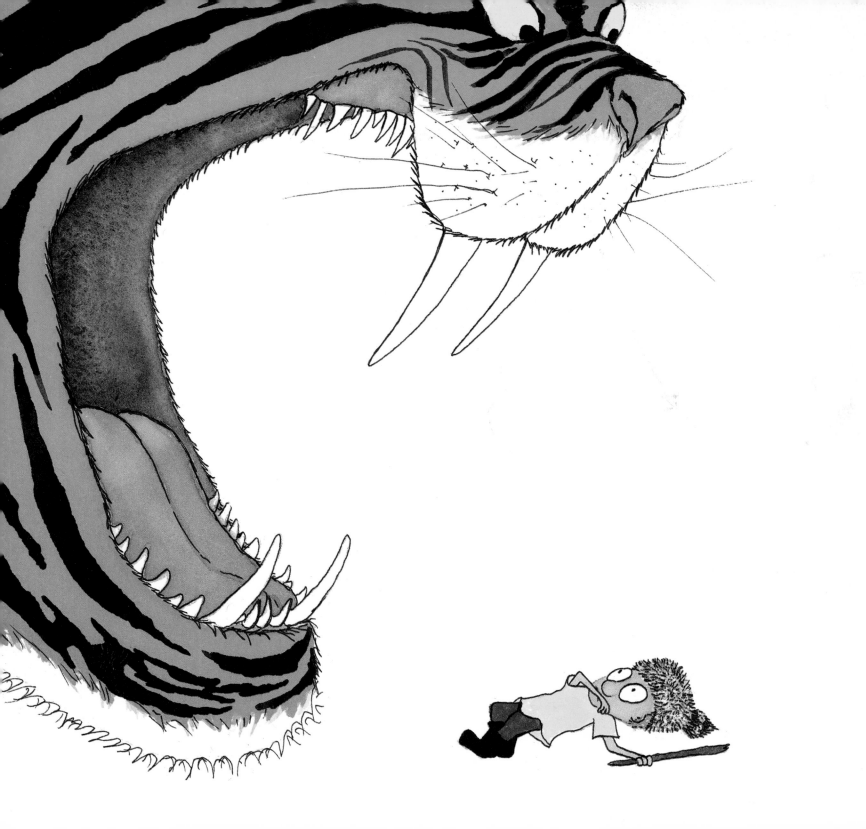

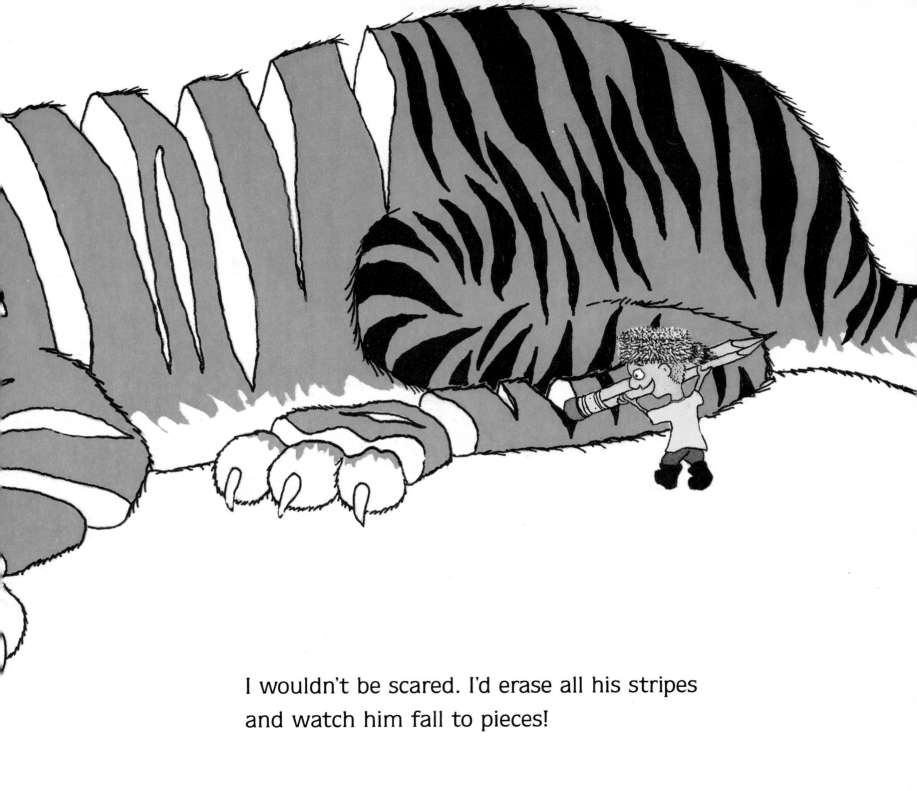

I wouldn't be scared. I'd erase all his stripes
and watch him fall to pieces!

*Hey!* the tracks go over to those bushes.

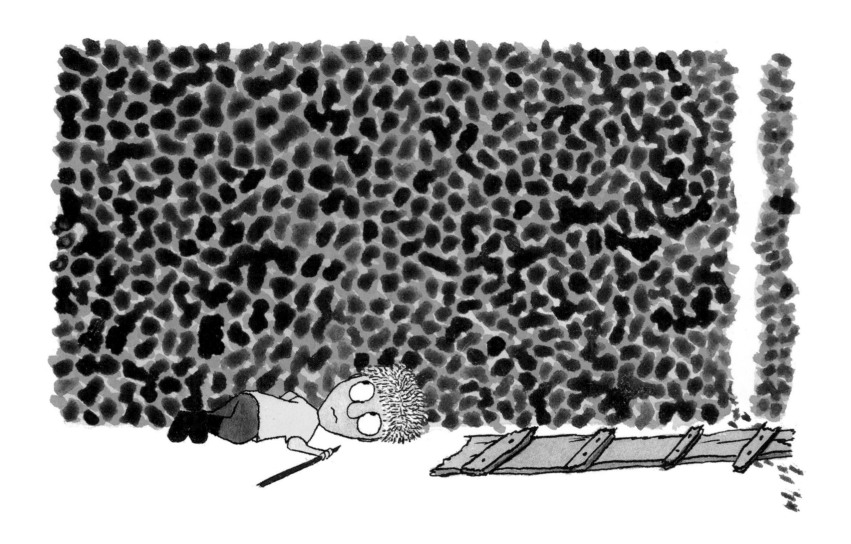

And something is moving behind them.

But I-I-I-I'm not scared!

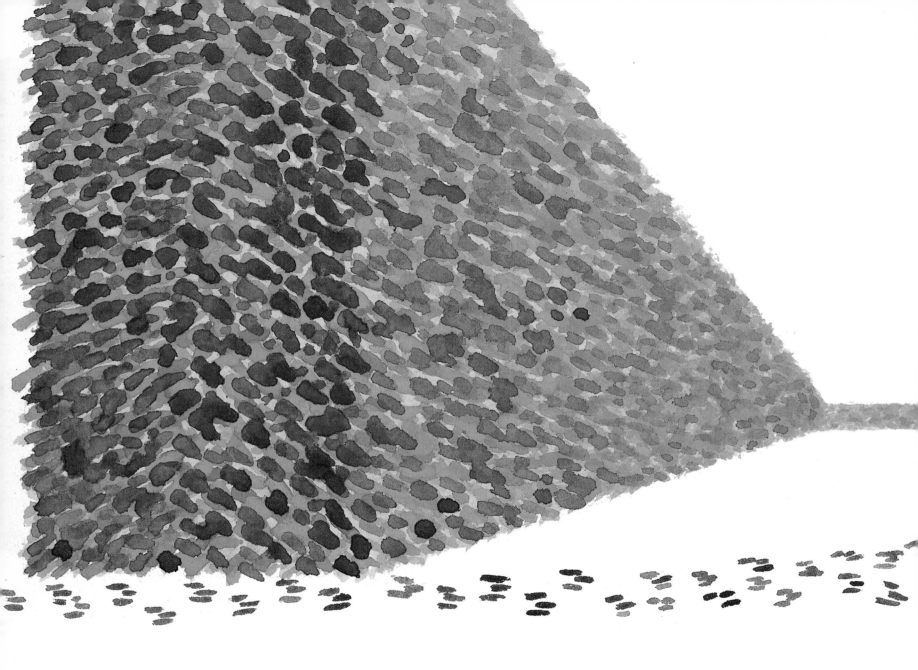

Well, it wasn't a dragon and it wasn't a snake or a spider or a gorilla or even a hungry tiger.

And I wasn't scared either.